How Many Cookies?

Learning to Subtract 1 From One-Digit Numbers

Judi Austin

Math for the REAL World™

Rosen Classroom™

New York

I have five cookies to share!

Jan ate one cookie. There are four cookies left.

Tom ate one cookie. There are three cookies left.

Jill ate one cookie. There are two cookies left.

Joe ate one cookie. There is one cookie left.

I ate one cookie. Now there are no cookies left.

Words to Know

one

two

three

four

five